rainbow

THE CIRCUS COMES TO TOWN

Written by Clive Hopwood
Illustrated by Paul Crompton

Published in Great Britain by World International Publishing Limited,
An Egmont Company, Egmont House P.O. Box 111, Great Ducie Street, Manchester M60 3BL.
Printed in Germany. ISBN 7235 1358 9

REPRINTED 1992

Bungle, George, Zippy and Geoffrey are coming home after a weekend away. They like to visit their friends.

Geoffrey opens the door.

There is a piece of paper lying on the floor. Bungle picks it up. He reads it.

"Oh no," he says.

"What's the matter, Bungle?" asks George.

"Look at this," says Bungle.
"What does it say?" asks Zippy.
George reads it out. *"Grand
Circus. One day only. The greatest
show on Earth."*

"Ooh good," says Zippy. "A circus! Lions and elephants and clowns."

"Acrobats and jugglers," says George.

"And the man on the flying trapeze," laughs Geoffrey.

"I love a circus," says Zippy.
"Can we go, Geoffrey?" asks George.
"I don't see why not," says Geoffrey. "When is it on?"

"We can't go," says Bungle.
"Why not?" asks Zippy.
Bungle shows him the piece of
paper. "It's too late," he says.

George looks at the piece of paper again. "Oh no! Yesterday! The circus is over," he says. "It's gone away. It says 'one day only'."

"We missed it," says Zippy sadly.
"Never mind," says Geoffrey. "Another time."
"Oh," says George. "And a circus would be such fun."
Everyone is unhappy.

That night Zippy, George and Bungle get ready for bed. They clean their teeth and put on their pyjamas. Geoffrey tucks them into their beds.

"I wish we could go to the circus," says George dreamily.
"So do I," says Zippy.
"And me," says Bungle as he closes his eyes.

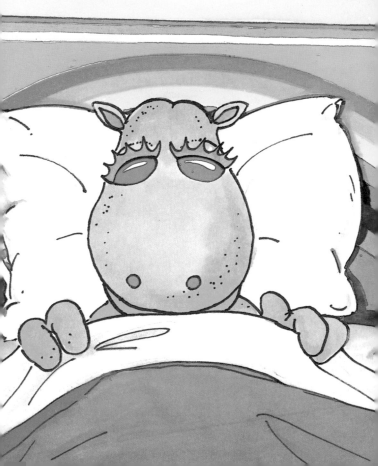

Next morning George wakes up smiling. Bungle and Zippy are still sad because they can't go to the circus.

They all sit down to breakfast.

Geoffrey looks at George. Then
he looks at Bungle and Zippy.
George is smiling. "You look happy
this morning, George," says
Geoffrey.

"I am happy," says George.
"Why are you so happy, George?" asks Zippy.
"A dream," says George. "A lovely dream."
"Tell us about it, George," says Bungle.

"It's a dream about the circus,"
says George. "There's a great big
tent."

"That's called the big top," says
Zippy.

"What's inside?" asks Bungle
excitedly.

"Inside the big top," George goes on, "is a big circle covered in sawdust."

"That's called a ring," says Bungle, "because it's round."

George tells them about his circus dream. There are lions and elephants. There are clowns and acrobats and jugglers. There is even a man on the flying trapeze.

Bungle, Zippy and Geoffrey listen to George's dream. They think it is a very good dream. It is almost as if they really are at the circus.

"I wish I could have a dream like that," says Zippy.

Bungle is thinking. "That gives me an idea," he says. "Come on, George and Zippy."

Later that morning Bungle hands Geoffrey a card. It is an invitation. It says, *"Special Circus. One day only. This afternoon in the garden."*

After lunch Geoffrey goes into the garden. There is a circle of rope laid on the lawn to make the circus ring.

Geoffrey sits back and watches.

George pretends to be a lion. He roars. Zippy is the lion-tamer.

Then Bungle juggles with some balls. He is the juggler.

George pretends to be an elephant and does tricks.

Bungle does a handstand. He is the acrobat.

Zippy wears a red nose and makes Geoffrey laugh. He is the clown.

Last of all, Bungle goes on the swing.

"I'm the man on the flying trapeze," he says.

At the end of the show they all bow.

Geoffrey claps and claps.
"Hurray for Zippy, George and
Bungle!" he says. "The best circus
in town!"

To show them how pleased he is,
he buys them all an ice-cream.